Dash!
LEVELED READERS

Level 1 – Beginning
Short and simple sentences with familiar words or patterns for children who are beginning to understand how letters and sounds go together.

Level 2 – Emerging
Longer words and sentences with more complex language patterns for readers who are practicing common words and letter sounds.

Level 3 – Transitional
More developed language and vocabulary for readers who are becoming more independent.

abdopublishing.com

Published by Abdo Zoom, a division of ABDO, PO Box 398166, Minneapolis, Minnesota 55439. Copyright © 2019 by Abdo Consulting Group, Inc. International copyrights reserved in all countries. No part of this book may be reproduced in any form without written permission from the publisher. Dash!™ is a trademark and logo of Abdo Zoom.

Printed in the United States of America, North Mankato, Minnesota.
052018
092018

Photo Credits: iStock, Seapics.com, Shutterstock
Production Contributors: Kenny Abdo, Jennie Forsberg, Grace Hansen, John Hansen
Design Contributors: Dorothy Toth, Neil Klinepier

Library of Congress Control Number: 2017917510

Publisher's Cataloging in Publication Data
Names: Murray, Julie, author.
Title: Mammals / by Julie Murray.
Description: Minneapolis, Minnesota : Abdo Zoom, 2019. | Series: Animal classes | Includes online resources and index.
Identifiers: ISBN 9781532122996 (lib.bdg.) | ISBN 9781532123979 (ebook) | ISBN 9781532124464 (Read-to-me ebook)
Subjects: LCSH: Mammals--Juvenile literature. | Mammalogy--Juvenile literature. |Speciation (Biology)--Juvenile literature. | Mammals--Behavior--Juvenile literature.
Classification: DDC 599--dc23

Table of Contents

Mammals 4

Mammal Traits 22

Glossary 23

Index 24

Online Resources 24

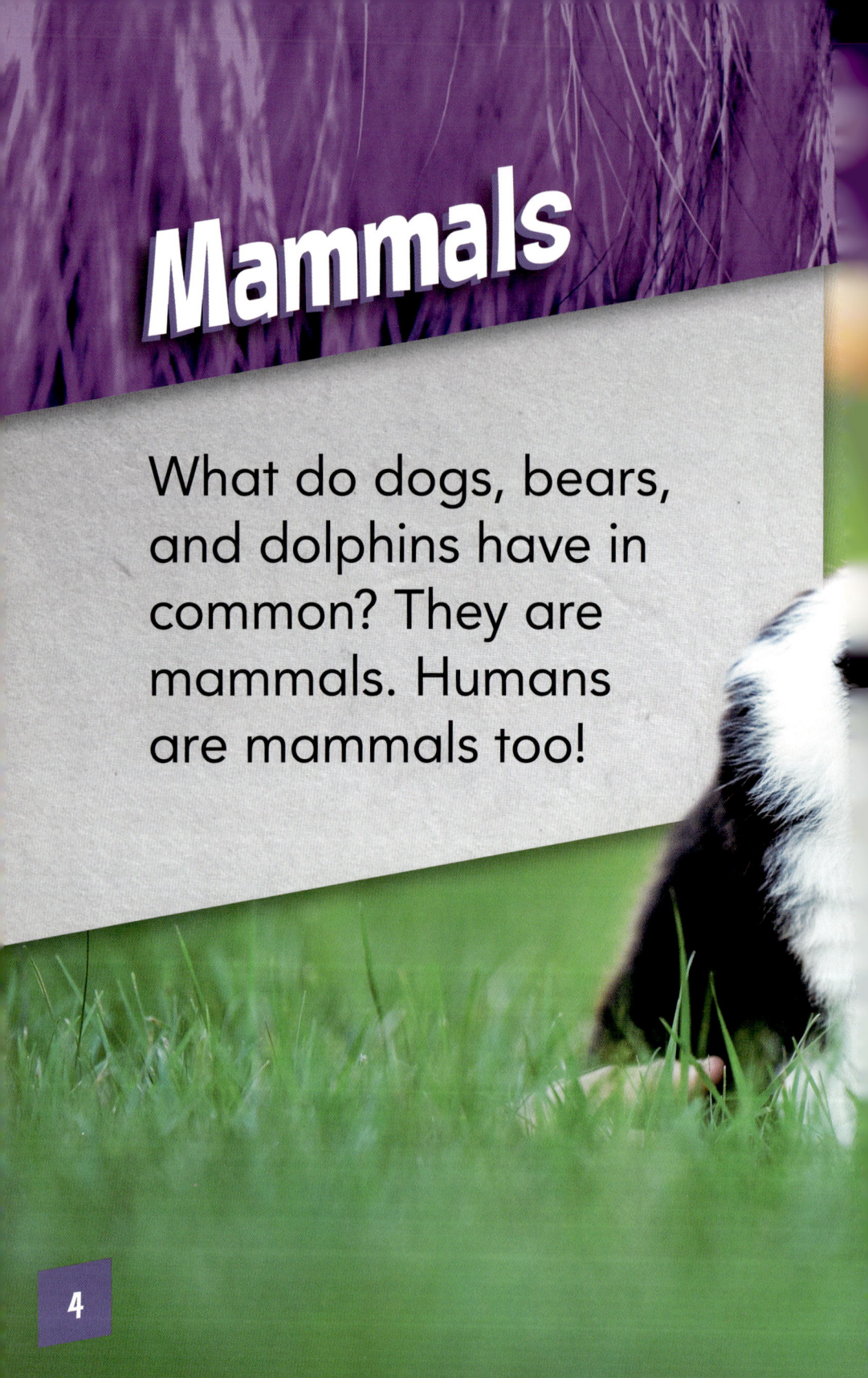

Mammals

What do dogs, bears, and dolphins have in common? They are mammals. Humans are mammals too!

Mammals live all over the world. Camels live in the desert.

Mammals are **warm-blooded**. Their bodies adapt to the outside temperature.

Mammals are **vertebrates**. Mice have tiny backbones.

Mammals breathe air. Their lungs allow them to breathe.

Mammals have hair.
Collies have long, soft hair.

Mammals give birth to live babies. Babies drink their mothers' milk and grow.

Some mammals eat meat. Others eat plants. Some eat both. Pandas eat **bamboo** plants.

The blue whale is the largest mammal. It can be 100 feet (30.5 m) long. It can weigh 260,000 pounds (117,934 kg)!

Mammal Traits

- Are **warm-blooded**
- Have a backbone
- Have lungs to breathe air
- Often covered in hair
- Give birth to live babies

Glossary

bamboo – a tropical grass that has hard, woody, hallow stems.

vertebrate – an animal that has a skeleton with a backbone inside its body.

warm-blooded – having a body temperature that remains steady and warm at different outside temperatures.

Index

babies 17

blue whale 21

camel 6

collie 15

food 17, 18

hair 15

human 4

lungs 13

mice 11

panda 18

range 6

reproduction 17

vertebrate 11

warm-blooded 8

Online Resources

Booklinks
NONFICTION NETWORK
FREE! ONLINE NONFICTION RESOURCES

To learn more about mammals, please visit **abdobooklinks.com**. These links are routinely monitored and updated to provide the most current information available.

MAR 2 9 2019